PRINCESS PULVERIZER

watch that witch!

PENGUIN WORKSHOP
An Imprint of Penguin Random House LLC, New York

Text copyright © 2019 by Nancy Krulik. Illustrations and logo copyright © 2019 by Penguin Random House LLC. All rights reserved. Published by Penguin Workshop, an imprint of Penguin Random House LLC, New York. PENGUIN and PENGUIN WORKSHOP are trademarks of Penguin Books Ltd, and the W colophon is a registered trademark of Penguin Random House LLC.
Printed in the USA.

Visit us online at www.penguinrandomhouse.com.

Library of Congress Cataloging-in-Publication Data is available upon request.

ISBN 9781524790929 (pbk)   10 9 8 7 6 5 4 3 2 1
ISBN 9781524790936 (hc)   10 9 8 7 6 5 4 3 2 1

NANCY KRULIK

Princess PULVERIZER

WATCH THAT WITCH!

art by Justin Rodrigues
based on original character designs by
Ben Balistreri

Penguin Workshop

For Danny, my partner in crime—NK

CHAPTER 1

"Step, step, lunge!" Lucas said as he took two steps to the right and then brandished a butter knife in the air. "Step, step . . . *whoops*!"

Bam!

Princess Pulverizer put her hand over her mouth with surprise as she watched her pal trip over a rock.

"Sorry," Lucas apologized to the rock.

Princess Pulverizer's cheeks turned purple. Her eyes began to tear up. She thought she might explode. But she refused to let out even a teeny tiny giggle. That wouldn't be nice. And Princess Pulverizer was trying hard to be nice these days.

"You're definitely getting better," Lucas's best friend, Dribble the dragon, assured him.

"You really think so?" Lucas wondered as he scrambled to his feet.

"You should try the riposte next," Dribble said. "You almost had that move down yesterday."

Princess Pulverizer knew what a riposte was—a counterattack against an opponent who had just lunged against you while you were fencing.

Only there wasn't anyone lunging at Lucas. He was fencing against empty air. With a butter knife.

And he was still losing.

Lucas held out the knife and gave it a quick thrust. The knife flew out of his hand and landed squarely in the middle of a pear hanging from a nearby tree.

The princess bit her upper lip to keep from laughing.

"Sir Lucas is the winner!" Dribble announced to an imaginary audience. "He has defeated his opponent! Huzzah!"

"*What* opponent?" Princess Pulverizer wondered.

"The tree, of course," Dribble replied. He picked the pricked pear from its branch. "This one's almost ripe. It will be delicious with a grilled gouda sandwich."

Princess Pulverizer licked her lips. That *did* sound yummy.

"I've never met anyone who tries harder than you," Dribble complimented Lucas. "You're going to be an amazing knight one day. They might even make you a king." The dragon bowed deeply. "All hail King Lucas! Long may he reign!"

The princess couldn't hold it in anymore. She laughed so hard, she snorted.

Drip. Drip. DROP!

Suddenly, completely out of nowhere, it began to rain. And not just little droplets. This was a *major* rainstorm! A *dragon-size* rainstorm.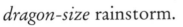

"I think you actually made it rain," Lucas told Dribble.

"I didn't mean to," Dribble said. "I was talking about the other kind of *reign*. Like when a king rules over his people."

"We knew what you meant," Princess

Pulverizer told him. "But *they* didn't!" She pointed to the dark rain clouds in the sky.

Plink. Plank. Ker-PLUNK. The raindrops were falling faster now.

"We have to find shelter," Princess Pulverizer shouted as she ran off in search of a place to get out of the rain.

"Yeah," Lucas agreed. "I don't want my armor to get any rustier." He took off after the princess.

"Hey! Wait for me!" Dribble called to his pals. "I'm right behind you."

"It's k-k-kind of c-c-c-old in here," Princess Pulverizer complained through chattering teeth as she and her friends gathered in the shelter of a large cave.

"It's dark, too," Lucas replied. "I've never liked caves."

"I'm hungry." Princess Pulverizer continued complaining. "How're those grilled cheese sandwiches coming?"

Dribble held up a cheddar cheese sandwich and let out a flame—medium heat. Perfect for toasting.

Well, *usually* perfect, anyway.

"It's no use," he told his friends. "The bread is too wet. It keeps falling apart."

"I've had enough of this!" Princess Pulverizer complained.

"Don't worry," Lucas said. "When the rain stops, we can buy a loaf of fresh bread."

"It's not the rain. Or the bread," Princess Pulverizer groused. "It's this Quest of Kindness. It's gone on long enough. I'm ready to go to Knight School."

"Oh, it's about the quest . . . again," Dribble said with a sigh.

"Yes, the quest again," Princess Pulverizer replied. "Isn't that why we're in the middle of nowhere in the pouring rain?"

"It's why *you're* out here," Dribble replied. "Lucas was already *in* Knight School."

"And then I was *out* of Knight School," Lucas added sadly. "I had to leave. The other boys made fun of me. It's not nice to call someone lily-livered."

"They wouldn't make fun of you *now*," Dribble assured him. "Not if they saw the way you helped battle that cheese monster and outsmarted those giant moles. You are definitely *not* lily-livered."

"Thanks," Lucas replied gratefully.

"The point is, I'm never going to get into Knight School at this rate," Princess Pulverizer continued. "I don't know why my father is making me do good deeds before he lets me go."

"You *know* why he's making you go on this Quest of Kindness," Lucas said. "You need to learn how to act in a more

knightly fashion before you can become a knight-in-training."

"But why did he order me to do *eight* good deeds?" Princess Pulverizer argued. "I've already completed four. That should be enough."

"*You've* completed four?" Dribble asked.

"I mean *we've* completed four," she admitted. "Together. Which shows that I've learned to work as part of a team.

That's part of being a good knight, right?"

"Definitely," Lucas agreed.

"And we've bravely risked our lives fighting ogres, trolls, and hairy underground beasts, haven't we?" she asked.

"To name just a few," Dribble agreed.

"And I've become really kind, right?" Princess Pulverizer added.

The sword of truth, a gift from the King of Salamistonia, began to quiver wildly by the princess's side. Okay, maybe that one wasn't *completely* true.

"Well, I'm kind*er*," Princess Pulverizer corrected herself. The sword lay still.

"You are," Lucas assured her.

"Then I should be allowed to enter Knight School with all the other knights-in-training *right now*!" she declared.

"Um . . . no," Dribble replied.

"Why not?" the princess demanded.

"Because knights must be patient," Dribble explained. "And you've got work to do in that department."

Princess Pulverizer glared at the dragon. But she couldn't argue.

"Hey, listen," Lucas said suddenly. "Do you hear that?"

"I don't hear anything," Princess Pulverizer said.

"Exactly," Lucas told her. "No more raindrops. I think the storm has passed."

"Let's get going," Princess Pulverizer exclaimed. "We've got things to do!"

"Things like buying fresh bread for sandwiches?" Dribble suggested.

"More like fighting bad guys and doing good deeds," Princess Pulverizer said.

"I'd rather have a grilled cheese sandwich," Lucas remarked as he followed the princess out into the sunlight.

"Wait for me!" Dribble lifted a shiny metal mace and carried it out of the cave.

The mace was a thank-you present from the King of Yabko-kokomo, who had wanted to show his gratitude to Princess Pulverizer and her friends for rescuing some of his subjects. It was a nice gift, but it was very heavy. Dribble was the only one of the trio strong enough to carry it for any distance.

"It sure is muddy out here," Dribble complained as he trudged under the weight of the mace along a wet dirt road. "The mud is squishing between my toes."

"We're almost at the top of this hill," Lucas assured his friend. "A few more steps and—" Lucas stopped midsentence. "Wow!" he exclaimed. "Look at that!"

Princess Pulverizer looked up to see a magnificent double rainbow, large enough to arc over the entire village below.

It had to be a sign. Something wonderful was waiting in that village. The princess just knew it.

CHAPTER 2

"It's so pretty here," Lucas said. "And happy. Everyone seems to be smiling."

"Great," Princess Pulverizer grumbled.

"What's wrong now?" Dribble asked.

"It's just that if everyone's happy, then no one needs my—I mean *our*—help," she explained. "We haven't seen one person who looks upset or angry."

"Oh, I know someone who is upset *and* angry," Dribble said.

"Really?" Princess Pulverizer asked excitedly. "Who?"

"Me!" Dribble exclaimed. "Do you think it's easy carrying this mace up and down these hills?" He plopped down on the ground. "I'm taking a rest."

"But we can't rest," Princess Pulverizer told him. "It's not like trouble is going to walk over and find *us*. We have to find *trouble*."

"Or . . . maybe we can wait here and ask a passerby if they know of anybody who needs help," Lucas suggested.

"Good idea!" Dribble exclaimed.

Princess Pulverizer couldn't really argue. Things hadn't been going so well doing it her way. She might as well try Lucas's plan. She sat down and waited for someone to walk by.

And waited. And waited.

"This isn't working," she complained.

"We've only been here for a few minutes," Dribble said. "You really *don't* have any patience, do you?"

"Here comes someone!" Lucas pointed toward two women lugging big buckets and a wagon full of stuffed bags up the hill. They had dirt on their faces and stains on their clothes. From the smell of things, it was clear they needed a good washing.

Princess Pulverizer wasn't about to let a bad stink stand in her way. "Hello," she said, leaping to her feet. "Are you in need of any help today?"

"Who, us?" the woman with the curls asked her. "Goodness no."

"We can carry our own washing and buckets," said the other woman, who wore her hair in braids. "We're the washerwomen of Starats. We're strong."

"Wait," Dribble interrupted. "*You* two clean people's clothes?"

"Of course," the curly-haired woman told him. "Somebody has to."

"Do you need any laundering?" the woman with braids asked. "We can get stains out of anything."

"You've heard about the leopard who fell in the laundry bucket, haven't you?"

the curly-haired woman asked. "He lost
his spots."

Her friend laughed. "Good one, Lily."

"Thanks, Millie," Lily replied.

"Do either of you know of anyone who
has a problem that needs fixing?" Princess
Pulverizer asked them.

"Fixings?" Millie repeated. "They serve
dinner with all the fixings at the inn."

"It's delicious," Lily added. "Chicken with stuffing, artichoke hearts, and—"

"Artie chokes hearts?" Millie asked. "Why would he want to do that?"

Lily laughed. "Anyway, the inn is that-a-way," she said, pointing left.

"No, it's this-a-way," Millie said, pointing right.

"Or it could be straight ahead," Lily said, pointing forward.

"Or back there." Millie bent down and pointed backward between her knees.

"Millie, we better get back to work," Lily said. "We have lots to do. We're lucky washing clothes is fun!"

Millie looked at the big bags of dirty clothes they were carting. "*Loads and loads* of fun," she agreed.

As the washerwomen walked off, Princess Pulverizer declared, "That was a waste of time."

"Not totally," Lucas pointed out. "We learned the name of the village. Starats."

"Big deal," Princess Pulverizer replied.

"I like to know where I am," Lucas insisted.

"I can tell you where we are," Princess

Pulverizer replied. "Right back where we started. *With no one to help*. We've rested enough. Let's get moving."

Dribble and Lucas didn't argue. They'd expected her to say that. The princess wasn't able to stay in one place for very long without getting antsy.

"You know, that chicken dinner sounded kind of yummy," Lucas said.

"Definitely," Dribble agreed. "If we pass that inn, maybe—"

WAAAAHHHHH!

Dribble was interrupted by loud cries coming from just up the road.

"Sounds like someone in need of help!" Princess Pulverizer exclaimed excitedly. "Don't worry, whoever you are," she cried out as she ran off. "Princess Pulverizer is coming to the rescue!"

"Do you think she forgets about us on purpose?" Dribble asked Lucas.

"There's a boy who's fallen in the middle of the road up ahead," Princess Pulverizer called back to Lucas and Dribble. "I can see him from here."

The princess hurried to the boy's aid. But before she could reach him, a woman appeared by his side. She had long, flowing dark hair and wore a bright blue gown.

Princess Pulverizer watched as the woman snapped her fingers and pulled a gingerbread cookie seemingly out of thin air.

The boy stopped crying. He smiled a little, stood up, and began to play with the gingerbread boy, making the cookie dance in his hands.

The woman in the blue gown waved her hand again and magically vanished.

"Where is the crying boy?" Dribble asked as he and Lucas arrived at Princess Pulverizer's side.

"You're too late," the princess said. "He's already happy again. See?"

"Well, that's good," Lucas said.

"What cheered him up?" Dribble wondered.

"This woman in a long blue dress appeared and gave him that gingerbread cookie," Princess Pulverizer explained.

"What woman?" Lucas asked. "I don't see anyone."

"I don't know where she went," Princess Pulverizer told him. "She appeared and then disappeared into thin air with a wave of her hand."

"Well, she's definitely gone now," Dribble said.

"Yes, it was very strange . . . ," Princess Pulverizer began. Then she stopped suddenly. "Wait, there she is again. Only now she's wearing a red gown. Boy, that was a quick change."

The princess watched as the dark-haired woman walked over to the boy once again and snapped her fingers in the air. Instantly, the gingerbread boy came alive.

"Whoa!" Dribble exclaimed.

"How'd she do that?" Lucas wondered.

"Magic, I guess." Princess Pulverizer wasn't very impressed. She was no stranger to magic. She'd seen the wicked Wizard of Wurst do much tougher tricks than bringing a cookie to life.

The child looked surprised as his gingerbread cookie dropped to the ground and began to dance on its own.

"That cookie can really boogie," Dribble said.

The little boy giggled at the sight of the dancing cookie. "Ha-ha-ha. Ha-ha—*WAH!*" The little boy let out a horrified cry. "That cookie bit my leg!" he wailed.

The woman in the red dress gave a haughty laugh, and without a word, disappeared again.

The gingerbread boy ran off down the road.

"A cookie biting a boy," Dribble said, surprised. "Now there's something you don't see every day."

"That's for sure," Princess Pulverizer agreed. She didn't know much about Starats. But it was safe to say this was no ordinary place.

CHAPTER 3

"OW OW *OW!*" Dribble let out a dragon-size cry and dropped to the ground.

Lucas came running over. "What's the matter?" he asked his friend nervously.

"It's my foot," Dribble told him. "It's starting to blister."

Dribble held up his right foot. Sure enough, there was a huge scaly green blister on the bottom.

"That looks bad," Lucas told Princess
Pulverizer.

"We can bandage it up," Princess
Pulverizer suggested.

"That won't do it," Dribble said. "I
have to rest. My heel needs to heal."

Lucas giggled. "Good one," he
complimented the dragon.

"But that could take days," Princess

Pulverizer said. "You saw what happened with that gingerbread cookie. There's something evil going on in this town, and we have to stop it."

"I can't move another inch," Dribble insisted. "That mace is heavy and I—"

"That's it!" Lucas exclaimed excitedly.

"*What's* it?" Dribble and Princess Pulverizer asked at the exact same time.

"The mace," Lucas repeated. "Don't you remember what the King of Yabko-kokomo said? The mace can heal the wounds of anyone who fights on the side of what is good and right."

Dribble's face brightened. "So all you have to do is wave that thing over my foot and I'll be good as new."

"Wait a minute," Princess Pulverizer said. "The king also said that if we try to use the mace's power on someone who is deceitful or evil, its magic will disappear."

Dribble's cheeks grew purple with anger. "Are you saying I'm deceitful or evil?" he demanded.

"Well, no," the princess said slowly. "But you aren't always nice. I just don't want to lose the magic in the mace. What if we need it for something important?"

"Are you saying my blister isn't important?" Dribble argued.

"Of course not," Princess Pulverizer assured him.

"No one can be good all the time," Lucas pointed out. "But Dribble is kind *most* of the time."

"I suppose it's worth a try," Princess Pulverizer finally agreed. She picked up the mace. Her knees buckled under its weight. "Whoa, this *is* heavy."

"I told you," Dribble said.

"Okay, mace, do your stuff!" Princess Pulverizer said as she waved the golden apple above Dribble's blister.

The three friends stared at Dribble's foot, waiting for something to happen.

Only nothing did.

A dragon-size purple tear streamed from Dribble's eye. "I don't get it," he said. "I'm a good guy. Or at least I try to be."

"You *are* a good guy," Lucas insisted. "That mace must be broken."

"Look!" Princess Pulverizer exclaimed. "Your blister is melting, Dribble!"

Dribble looked down. Sure enough, the blister had dissolved. "It's good to know I'm not a rotten dragon, after all," Dribble said.

"We knew that already," Lucas told him. "Didn't we?"

"Sure," the princess agreed. "Now let's get moving. I want to find out what's going on around here."

But before the dragon could scramble up onto his newly healed foot, the sound of loud, cackling laughter came from down the road.

"Here come those washerwomen again," Princess Pulverizer said.

"You recognize their laughs?" Lucas asked her.

The princess shook her head.

"I recognize their *smell*," she said. "They really need to bathe."

"Well, hello," Lily greeted Princess Pulverizer and her pals.

"Fancy meeting you here," Millie added.

Princess Pulverizer looked at the huge bundles of laundry the washerwomen were dragging. It seemed as though they washed the clothes of everyone in the village. Which meant the washerwomen had to *know* everyone in the village!

"Say," Princess Pulverizer remarked to

Millie and Lily. "Would you two happen to know a woman with long dark hair who knows a bit of magic?"

Millie and Lily looked at each other.

"Long dark hair you say?" Lily asked.

"Knows a bit of magic?" Millie wondered.

Suddenly the two washerwomen began reciting a poem.

> *"If two witches were watching two watches,*
> *which witch would watch which watch?"*

Lucas looked at them curiously. "I don't get it," he said.

"*I* get it," Princess Pulverizer said. "They are *two* different women. That's why they were wearing two different dresses. And they're *witches*, which is why they can disappear into thin air and make cookies dance. They might look alike, but

‹41›

they act really differently. Like one witch gave the boy a cookie, and the other one brought the cookie to life and laughed when it bit that boy. You have to *watch* them to see the difference."

"The witches are twins," Millie explained. "Anna is the kind one. She uses her magic to bring joy to Starats, because she wants this to be a peaceful place. Happy people rarely fight."

"Her sister, Elle, is very selfish," Lily continued. "She has no problem taking whatever she wants, no matter who it hurts. The more people fight, the easier it is for her to swoop in and become more powerful. Divide and conquer. That's Elle's motto."

"I think she enjoys making people feel bad," Millie added.

Princess Pulverizer nodded. Considering how Elle had laughed when the gingerbread cookie bit the boy, that was probably true.

"Doesn't anybody ever fight back against Elle?" Lucas asked.

Millie shook her head. "Everyone is too afraid of her," she explained.

"*Anna* isn't afraid," Lily disagreed. "She tries to fix the messes Elle makes. But their powers are equal. There isn't much Anna can do."

"I guess there isn't any real way to defeat an evil witch," Dribble said.

"Well, there's a rumor that if Elle were to look in the reflecting pool near the bell tower, she would turn to stone," Millie said. "*That* would stop her."

"Right in her tracks," Lily agreed.

"The reflecting pool doesn't show what a person looks like on the outside, it shows their true *inner* being," Millie explained. "Elle already has a heart of stone. One look at her inner ugliness and the rest of her would turn to stone as well."

"So why hasn't anyone tried that?" Princess Pulverizer asked.

"Elle knows the legend," Lily pointed out. "She won't go anywhere near that reflecting pool."

The princess nodded. That made sense.

"We'd better get going," Millie said as she fished a wet sock out of her bucket. "See this guy? He's looking for his *sole* mate. And it could take a while to find it."

"Don't you two ever get tired of washing?" Dribble wondered.

"Nah." Lily shook her head. "We'd

never throw in the towel."

"It would just mean more laundry to do," Millie added with a laugh.

As the washerwomen wandered off, Lucas shot Princess Pulverizer a nervous look. "Maybe we should look for an act of kindness to do in a town where there are no evil witches."

"Are you kidding?" Princess Pulverizer replied. "Ridding Starats of an evil witch would be an amazingly good deed. And every good deed brings me one step closer to getting enrolled in Knight School. You know how tired I am of waiting for *that* to happen."

"Oh, we know, Princess," Dribble assured her.

"Hey, did you hear that?" Lucas said nervously.

"Hear what?" Princess Pulverizer asked.

"There's something rustling in those bushes," Lucas said. "Someone's hiding in there."

"It's probably just a squirrel," Princess Pulverizer replied. "Now come on. Let's get looking for those witches."

"I'm not so sure that's a good idea," Lucas said. "It would be pretty hard for three normal travelers to defeat a witch."

Dribble looked at the timid former knight-in-training and the princess who longed to be a knight. Then he thought about his own dream: to use his fire to be a chef, instead of burning down villages like most dragons. "I wouldn't exactly call us normal," he said.

"We're better than normal," Princess Pulverizer insisted. "We're smart, and brave, and we have something neither of those witches has."

"What's that?" Lucas asked her nervously.

"The power of three!" Princess Pulverizer shouted. "When we work together, no one can stop us!"

CHAPTER 4

"That's a catchy tune," Dribble said as he and his friends entered the village square. "Bagpipes always make me want to dance." The big dragon began tapping his toes. He moved his feet to the beat. The ground shook beneath him.

"Earthquake!" someone in the crowd shouted.

"No! *Dragon!*" another person screamed.

Everyone in the crowd ran off, leaving the bagpipe player without his audience.

Dribble stopped his toe-tapping. "Why do people always do that?" he asked sadly.

The bagpipe player started to run, too. But Lucas stopped him. "You don't have to go," he assured the musician. "Dribble won't hurt you. He just wants to dance."

The bagpipe player didn't look so certain.

Suddenly a woman with long dark hair, wearing a purple gown, strolled over to the bagpipe player.

"Is that Anna or Elle?" Lucas whispered to Princess Pulverizer.

"I'm not sure," Princess Pulverizer admitted. "But I think there's a test we can give her. I heard somewhere that truly evil people cannot look you in the eye when they speak to you." Princess Pulverizer shrugged. "It's worth a try."

"Good sir, would you play a little tune for us?" the witch in the purple dress asked the bagpipe player. "Please?"

Princess Pulverizer walked over to the witch. "Do you like bagpipe music?" she asked, staring her in the eye.

"Love it!" the woman exclaimed. She stared right back at the princess. Satisfied, Princess Pulverizer smiled and hurried back to her friends. "That's Anna," she whispered confidently. "She looked me right in the eye."

"And she said *please*," Lucas pointed out. "A bad witch wouldn't have good manners."

Lucas pulled out his fife and began playing along with the bagpipes.

The squeaky fife and the high-pitched bagpipe were really making Princess Pulverizer's head pound. But she seemed to be the only one who felt that way. Dribble, Lucas, and Anna were all having a great time.

The bagpipe player picked up the tempo.

Lucas played faster.

Dribble twirled in a circle.

And Anna waved her hands wildly in the air.

POP! Suddenly the bagpipe burst like a giant balloon right in the bagpipe player's face.

"Now *that's* entertainment!" Anna let out a scornful laugh.

Except it *wasn't* Anna. Princess Pulverizer was sure of that. A kind witch would never make a musical instrument burst. And she would never laugh in someone's face. The woman in purple *had* to be Elle.

Lucas must have realized that, too, because he was now hiding behind Dribble.

"Why would you laugh at this poor musician?" Dribble asked her. "How could anyone be so cruel?"

"I was doing you a favor," Elle snarled. "No one really likes bagpipe music."

"That's true," Princess Pulverizer agreed.

The princess regretted the words the minute they slipped out of her mouth. The poor bagpipe player looked as though he might cry. Quickly he gathered up what was left of his instrument, and raced away.

"I'm sorry," the princess called after him. "It was just a joke."

"You're my kind of girl." Elle wrapped her arm around Princess Pulverizer's shoulder. "I bet you have a lot of ambition."

Princess Pulverizer nodded. "I want to—"

"Shhh . . . ," Dribble warned. "Don't tell her anything."

"I need someone like you to help me out," Elle continued, ignoring Dribble. "How would you like to come work for me?"

Princess Pulverizer looked at her in surprise. "Why would I want to do that?"

"Because one day, I'm going to rule all of Starats," Elle replied.

"Who rules Starats now?" Princess Pulverizer asked her.

"No one, actually," Elle said. "Not since my mother and father died. The next ruler should be their firstborn. But since Anna and I are twins, we're *both* the firstborn."

"One of you must have been born first,"

Dribble said. "Even if it was just a minute before."

"I say I was born first," Elle told him. "And Anna says she was. But nobody knows. Our birth certificates seem to have disappeared."

Dribble gave Elle a suspicious look. "Disappeared?" he asked. "Just like that?"

Elle didn't answer the dragon. Instead she continued speaking directly to Princess Pulverizer. "Anna doesn't even think Starats needs a leader. She thinks everyone is equal. But we know better, don't we? Some people are born leaders."

Princess Pulverizer nodded. That was definitely true. She certainly felt *she* had been born to lead.

"Don't worry about Anna," Elle continued. "I certainly don't. I *will* rule this place. And when I do, you'll want to be on my good side."

"Princess Pulverizer will never work for you!" Lucas insisted.

Elle ignored him. "I need someone to sneak around town and make sure people aren't plotting against me," she told Princess Pulverizer. "Imagine yourself leaping down from trees to surprise our enemies. How fun would *that* be?"

"The element of surprise *is* important," Princess Pulverizer murmured.

"You're not actually considering this, are you?" Dribble asked her.

"Me?" Princess Pulverizer replied. "No, of course not. I was just saying—"

"Didn't I hear that you're tired of waiting to go to Knight School?" Elle continued.

"Where did you hear *that*?" Dribble asked suspiciously.

"Um . . . well . . . everyone's talking about it," Elle said.

The sword of truth shook. The princess tried to ignore it. But Lucas had seen it move. "That's not true," he insisted. "You were spying on us from the bushes while we were talking. I knew someone was hiding there."

"What does it matter how I heard it? What matters is that the princess is right. She shouldn't have to wait a moment longer. Come work for me, and I'll dub you a Royal Knight of Starats. Immediately."

"*Immediately?*" Princess Pulverizer repeated.

Elle nodded. "No more good deeds."

"Do you have the authority to do that?" Dribble asked.

"Who's gonna stop me?" Elle shot

Princess Pulverizer an evil grin. "So, what do you say? Do you want to be a knight—*right now*?"

"A knight?" Princess Pulverizer repeated. Was it possible? She'd wanted this for so long. And now Elle was offering her the chance.

"I know you would never do that," Dribble insisted, interrupting Princess Pulverizer's thoughts. "Being a knight at your father's Skround Table is an honor," Dribble continued. "But being a knight here, serving *her*, would not be honorable at all."

Princess Pulverizer frowned. Of course she knew that. Every night as she fell asleep, she pictured herself sitting beside the knights of Empiria at the Skround Table, talking of brave deeds.

"A knight's a knight," Elle insisted. "It doesn't matter at what table you sit."

Princess Pulverizer looked from Elle to her friends. She wasn't sure what to do.

Elle waved her hand in the air. "To sweeten my offer, I will give you this." She opened her fist to reveal a golden brooch with a shimmering opal stone in the center.

The princess stared at the pin. The stone seemed to change colors as the light hit it.

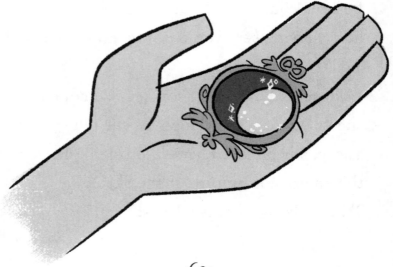

"An opal! The stone of tears!" Lucas exclaimed. "Don't touch it."

"Go ahead, try it on," Elle urged the princess.

"Don't trust her," Dribble warned Princess Pulverizer.

"It's no big deal," the princess told him. "It's just a pin."

"I don't like anything about this," Dribble said. "If you put that brooch on—"

Princess Pulverizer wasn't listening to Dribble anymore. She'd already put the golden opal pin on, right over her heart. The stone shimmered blue and pink in the sunlight.

"That looks lovely on you," Elle complimented her.

Princess Pulverizer looked down at the shimmering stone and then stared vacantly back at Elle. "Thank you, my queen," she said with a deep curtsy.

"Did she just call her 'my queen'?" Lucas whispered to Dribble.

"You are welcome, my dear knight," Elle replied.

"She's not *your* dear," Dribble said. "And she's not a knight."

"Careful," Elle warned him. "Argue with me again, and I'll turn you into a lizard."

Dribble gulped.

"Come," Elle said, leading Princess Pulverizer away. "I have many tasks for you to perform in my name."

"I shall do whatever you ask," Princess Pulverizer said.

"What just happened?" Lucas asked Dribble as the princess and witch walked off.

"It's that pin," the dragon answered. "Princess Pulverizer must be under a spell. Come on, we have to go."

"Where?" Lucas wondered.

"Wherever *they're* going," Dribble replied. "We have to keep an eye on the princess. And we have to figure out a way to stop this."

CHAPTER 5

Princess Pulverizer hid quietly on a tree branch and watched as a tailor dropped a doublet into a vat of steaming red dye in the yard behind his shop.

The princess's heart pounded quickly as she watched the man stir the short padded jacket around in the giant tub. This was her first task since becoming a knight of Starats. She wanted it to go smoothly.

"How's that doublet coming, Alistair?" asked another tailor, who was busy dyeing a tunic a rich royal blue next door in his own yard.

"Not bad, Maddox," Alistair replied. "I'm just going to leave it here to soak while I finish hemming a cloak for Lord Hucklebury. I'll be right back."

"Okay." Maddox returned to stirring his bucket of blue dye.

Princess Pulverizer was very impressed by the doublet Alistair was dyeing. From her perch in the tree, she could see the jacket had been made with great care. It would be a shame for it to be ruined.

Just then, the sun peeked out from behind a cloud. The bright light hit the opal brooch on Princess Pulverizer's chest. The pink-and-blue stone shimmered, catching the princess's eye. A dull look came over her.

Maybe it wouldn't be a shame for the doublet to be ruined, after all.

The princess took a flying leap into Alistair's yard. She landed silently, thanks to the ruby ring she wore. The ring had been a gift from the Queen of Shmergermeister. It gave whoever wore it the ability to move without making a sound.

Quickly Princess Pulverizer dumped a package of bright yellow saffron powder into the giant tub and then hid behind a tree.

A moment later, Alistair returned to his yard to check on the doublet sitting in the large vat of dye. He took one look and his face turned bright red.

"How could you do this?" he shouted at Maddox.

"Do what?" Maddox asked.

"Turn this dye from red to orange!" Alistair shouted.

"I did no such thing," Maddox insisted.

"Well, it didn't do it to itself." Alistair pulled the doublet from the dye and hung it on the line. "Look at this. It's bright orange. It's supposed to be red."

"It's not my fault," Maddox replied.

Angrily, Alistair dipped a clay cup into the orange dye. He stormed over to his neighbor's yard and spilled the orange liquid into Maddox's vat.

Maddox's face turned purple. So did the dye in his vat.

"Look what you did to this tunic!" Maddox exclaimed.

Maddox pulled a gray-purple tunic from his vat and hung it on the line. "It's ruined!" he cried out. "Even if I tried to add more blue dye, it would never be the right shade."

Maddox went to his workbench, grabbed a glass of green dye, and splashed it on the orange doublet Alistair had hung on *his* line. "Take that!" Maddox shouted.

"Take *this*!" Alistair splashed pink dye on Maddox's purple tunic.

Princess Pulverizer grinned as she watched the tailors splash color after color into each other's yards. Red. Orange. Yellow. Green. Blue. Violet. *What a mess*.

Yes! This was going exactly the way Elle had intended when she'd given Princess Pulverizer her orders. The men were angry. Their friendship was ruined. And so were the clothes they had hoped to sell.

"You knew I needed to sell this doublet to fix the rain damage in my cottage. Thatched roofs don't come free," Alistair shouted angrily at Maddox.

"Well, it's not like I'm rolling in silver coins," Maddox argued back. "I needed to sell this tunic to buy food."

For a moment, Princess Pulverizer felt terrible about the trouble she'd caused. But then, the sun shone directly on the opal pin. The blue-and-pink stone sparkled. And for some unknown reason, Princess Pulverizer no longer felt bad for the men at all. In fact, she let out a small giggle of delight.

"Did you just laugh at me?" Alistair demanded.

"No. *You* laughed at *me*," Maddox insisted. "And there's nothing funny about this. Where will I get the money to feed my children now?"

Princess Pulverizer grinned. She knew there was someone who could loan Maddox and Alistair all the silver they needed—Elle!

And once the wicked witch had loaned them the money, they would be in her debt. It was a heavy price, but one they'd surely pay.

Princess Pulverizer was about to leave and report her success to Elle when a woman with long dark hair strolled into the yard. Was it Elle? Or was it Anna?

The princess watched whichever witch it was wave her hands in the air. The blotches of colors on the doublet and the tunic began moving magically until they formed vibrant rainbow-shaped patterns on the cloth.

"Amazing," Alistair exclaimed.

"Marvelous," Maddox agreed.

A moment later, a nobleman in his carriage pulled up near the two tailor shops. He strutted into Maddox's yard. "I am here for my blue tunic," he announced.

Princess Pulverizer choked back a laugh. That nobleman was going to be angry.

Maddox gulped. "Well . . . you see . . . there was a bit of a problem with the dye, sir," he stammered.

"Don't be so modest," the witch told Maddox. She smiled at the nobleman. "These two craftsmen have worked together to create unique fashions. Look at the rainbows of color they have created. There are no finer pieces of clothing anywhere in Starats."

The nobleman studied the clothing hanging on the lines. "I will take them

both." He pulled out four gold coins.
"And I will buy any other such outfits you
two can create together."

Princess Pulverizer couldn't believe it.
She'd followed Elle's instructions exactly.
Maddox and Alistair should have been at
each other's throats. Instead they were
shaking hands, vowing to
work as a team.

GRRR. Princess
Pulverizer now
knew for sure that
the witch who had
helped the tailors
was that goody-
goody, Anna.
And she
had ruined
everything.

CHAPTER 6

"I don't know why my sister has to spoil all my fun!" Elle complained later that afternoon. Princess Pulverizer had met up with her in the center of town with news of the failed task. "You need to watch out for Anna. If you see her nearby, wait until she leaves before you do your next knightly task."

Something in Princess Pulverizer's mind questioned whether the task she had been

given could really be described as knightly.
But as the sunlight bounced off the golden
brooch on Princess Pulverizer's chest, she
caught a glimpse of the opal. Immediately,
all her doubts and questions disappeared.

"I am your humble servant," she said.
"Let me do another job in your honor."

"I'm in the mood for strawberries," Elle
replied with sinister grin. "Go to the farm
by the fork in the road, and bring me the
farmer's latest crop."

"His *whole* crop?" Princess Pulverizer asked.

"Every single berry," Elle replied. "And do not offer him anything in return. I always take whatever I want. So shall you."

"Yes, ma'am," Princess Pulverizer said.

"And remember what I told you," Elle added. "Before you approach that farmer, make sure my sister is nowhere to be seen."

Huff puff. Huff puff.

Princess Pulverizer panted heavily as she made her way up the last hill before the fork in the road. This knight thing sure wasn't what she thought it would be. She had no horse to carry her. No suit of glorious armor. No shield with the crest of Starats emblazoned upon it. Nothing—except a little gold brooch.

Princess Pulverizer looked down at the pin. The opal stone glimmered up at her. A dull look came over the princess as she picked up her pace. She could no longer think of anything but following Elle's command.

As she approached the farm, Princess Pulverizer looked around for any sign of Anna. But there was nothing. Not even a footprint in the dirt. The coast was clear.

"I COME IN THE NAME OF ELLE!" the princess bellowed.

The farmer looked up, surprised. "What can I do for you, m'lady?" he asked Princess Pulverizer kindly.

"I'm not a lady. I'm a *knight*. And I have come for all your strawberries!"

"All of them? Wow!" the farmer said excitedly. "Give me a minute. It will take some time to add up the cost for so many bushels of berries."

"I'm not paying you for them," Princess Pulverizer said. "Elle *never* pays. And neither do I, her faithful knight."

Just then Dribble and Lucas came huffing and puffing up the hill.

Princess Pulverizer

stared at them. "What are you doing here?" she demanded.

"Following you," Lucas told her.

"We heard what you just said," Dribble added angrily. "You can't just take whatever you want. How is this farmer supposed to make a living if you steal his berries?"

"He can plant a *different* crop," Princess Pulverizer said. "Something Elle doesn't like as much as strawberries."

"What crop?" the farmer asked her.

"*Beets* me." Princess Pulverizer laughed.

"Why don't you tell that joke to the cows?" Dribble scoffed. "They might find it a-*moo*-zing. But we don't. There's nothing funny about stealing."

"I'd like to stay and chat, but I have to get these berries to my boss," Princess

Pulverizer said. She picked up ten large bushels of berries, each one stacked on top of the other. "These are heavy."

"Please don't take them all," the farmer begged her.

Princess Pulverizer ignored the farmer's pleas. Instead she began walking away, her knees buckling under the weight of the buckets of berries.

MEOW! Just then a black cat darted out into the road.

Uh-oh! The princess was well aware that if a black cat crossed your path, it meant bad luck. She didn't need any of that.

Quickly, Princess Pulverizer turned to step out of the cat's way. But as she did, she tripped over a rock and fell. The berries tumbled to the ground and landed in the mud. Many of them were squished underneath her.

"My berries!" the farmer exclaimed.

"Elle's berries!" Princess Pulverizer shouted.

There was a gust of wind, and suddenly the cat was gone. In her place stood a woman with dark hair and a long green dress.

The princess gulped. Was this Anna or Elle?

The witch waved her hand in the air. Instantly, ten jars of sweet strawberry jam appeared where the spilled berries once had been.

The witch smiled kindly. "I just love strawberry jam, don't you?" she asked. "You can sell these at market."

"Thank you, Anna," the farmer said.

The princess suspected the farmer was right. This witch, who had done a good deed, had to be Anna.

"As for you," Anna scolded Princess Pulverizer. "Be gone. We have no use for evil here."

"I'll just take those jars and be on my way," Princess Pulverizer replied. "I'm certain *Elle* will enjoy them."

"You'll have to plow through Lucas and me first," Dribble warned her.

"You'll have to get past me as well," Anna added. "And I assure you, you don't want to try *that*."

The princess looked at her two former friends, the farmer, and the witch. No way could she fight the power of *four*. Slowly she turned and walked away.

Suddenly, Princess Pulverizer felt very alone. And afraid. Because there was no telling what Elle might do when she heard she had failed. *Again.*

CHapteR 7

It sure is hot in here.

That was all Princess Pulverizer could
think as she slipped into her very first suit
of armor. The sun warmed the copper and
steel, keeping all the heat inside. She'd
only worn the suit a few minutes and
already she was drenched in sweat. She
couldn't imagine what it would feel like
once she put the helmet on.

It wasn't easy to walk in, either. Wearing

a full suit of armor wasn't anything like
Princess Pulverizer
had imagined.

But the princess
didn't dare complain.
She was being careful
not to anger Elle.
The evil witch had
been furious enough
with her after the
strawberry disaster.

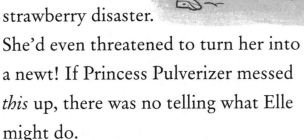

She'd even threatened to turn her into
a newt! If Princess Pulverizer messed
this up, there was no telling what Elle
might do.

So instead, Princess Pulverizer sighed
through her discomfort, glancing at
the field where that day's jousting
competitions were going to take place and

quietly asked, "Are you sure this is what armor is supposed to feel like? I can hardly move."

Elle rolled her eyes. "Why do I work with amateurs?" she shouted angrily to no one in particular. "This is *jousting* armor, you fool. It's much heavier than normal armor. I'd have had it made even heavier, but the armorer said the horse might collapse under the weight."

Thank goodness for that armorer.

"Now, I have something special for you!" Elle sounded very excited. "A shield! With my personal crest."

The witch handed Princess Pulverizer a large round shield, with a skeleton head carved in its center.

"*That's* your crest?" Princess Pulverizer asked.

"I designed it myself," Elle replied, smoothing the skirt of her blue-and-white-striped gown. "Isn't it lovely?"

Lovely wasn't exactly the word Princess Pulverizer was thinking of. Still, she answered, "Yes. It's great. Thank you."

Elle beamed. "I knew you would like it. Now come on. We have to head over to the center of the field so you can pick your lance. And you better choose well. Because there's no way I . . . I mean *you* . . . are going to lose this joust. Do you understand?"

Princess Pulverizer nodded nervously.

As she followed Elle through the wooden gate and over to the center of the list field where the joust was to take place, the princess felt her heart pounding with excitement. She'd sat in the boxes with her father many times during jousting contests. But this was so much better. Soon she would hear the cheers of the crowd as she rode toward her opponent and broke her lance against his shield. Or even better, knocked him from his horse.

"*You're* riding in this joust?"

Dribble's voice knocked the daydream from Princess Pulverizer's mind. She looked up and saw Dribble and Lucas standing beside a woman who looked just like Elle. Beside them was a tall man in shiny armor. He had a huge white-and-blue plume shooting out from his helmet.

"I wish you the best of luck," Anna told Princess Pulverizer sweetly. She smoothed the skirt of her white-and-blue-striped gown. "It will be a fine match. My knight, Sir Stately, is a skilled rider." She patted

the knight on the back.

"I hope he's a skilled *loser*, too," Elle told her sister. "Because that's what is going to happen to him."

Now Princess Pulverizer understood why Elle had been so anxious for her to win this match. There was no way she wanted to lose to her sister—again.

The marshal walked over to Princess Pulverizer and Sir Stately. He held out a selection of lances. "Choose your weapons," he said.

Princess Pulverizer immediately grabbed for the largest lance. But it was difficult to control because her hands were so small—she was just a kid after all. So she returned it, and grabbed a much smaller lance instead.

"Don't choose that one," Lucas warned her. "You'll have to ride too close to Sir Stately to break it on his shield. It's dangerous."

Princess Pulverizer gave him a haughty stare. "Have you ever been in a joust?"

"No," he admitted. "I was always too scared to get up on a horse."

Princess Pulverizer laughed in his face. "Then what do you know?"

"You sure have gotten mean," Lucas

said, his eyes filling with tears.

Princess Pulverizer felt a slight twinge of guilt. Lucas had been her friend. And he'd saved her more than once on her Quest of Kindness.

But that no longer mattered. She wasn't on that quest any longer.

"Take your stations!" the marshal announced.

Princess Pulverizer walked across the field to her chocolate-brown stallion. She placed one leg in the stirrup and leaped up onto the horse, then waved to the crowd.

BOOOOOOOO!!!!!

Whoa! The princess hadn't expected that. Why would the crowd boo her? They didn't even *know* her.

Then again, they knew Elle was evil. And they knew that Princess Pulverizer worked for Elle. So clearly they figured Princess Pulverizer was evil, too.

Well, Princess Pulverizer would show them. They'd be *cheering* her soon enough. She had this joust in the bag. She'd been to more contests than this Sir Stately guy could ever imagine. Okay, she had been in the stands, but still . . . All she had to do was exactly what she'd seen other jousting knights do. *Easy peasy.*

"The rules are as follows," the marshal announced to the crowd. "There will be three rounds. The knights receive one point for breaking their lance on their opponent's shield, and two points for knocking their opponent to the ground."

Princess Pulverizer smiled. She was going to knock Sir Stately right off his horse. Nothing less.

"Let the joust begin!" the marshal shouted.

"Giddyap!" Princess Pulverizer shouted as she kicked her horse with her heels.

Princess Pulverizer's stallion took off, heading in Sir Stately's direction.

Sir Stately's stallion took off, heading in Princess Pulverizer's direction.

The crowd cheered.

"Closer! Get closer!" The princess heard Elle's voice above everyone else's. "You cannot let him win!"

Don't worry, Princess Pulverizer thought. *He's not winning.* She steered the horse closer toward Sir Stately's path and held her lance out.

Sir Stately held his lance out, too.

Whoa. Sir Stately's lance was much longer than Princess Pulverizer's, and yet

he seemed to have it completely under his control.

Princess Pulverizer couldn't even keep her *small* lance still. It was shaking in her hand.

"Knock him to the ground," Elle shouted over the crowd. "Get closer."

Elle was right. The only way Princess Pulverizer could knock Sir Stately from his stallion would be to come up right against him. She yanked the reins to the left.

Her horse turned closer to Sir Stately.
And closer. And even closer still.

The princess was now so close, she
could see the whites of Sir Stately's eyes
through his visor.

THUD!

Something slammed Princess Pulverizer
right in the chest. She sensed her horse's
legs buckling beneath her. She felt herself
falling. And then everything went dark.

CHAPTER 8

"Get up, you fool!" The first sound Princess Pulverizer heard when she opened her eyes was Elle's bellowing, angry voice.

Neigh. Neigh. The second sound was the whimpering of her injured horse.

"She can't get up. Don't you see she's injured?" The third sound was Dribble's voice. He seemed rather concerned.

The princess struggled to look up

through the eyehole in her visor. She could just about make out Elle, Anna, Lucas, and Dribble all standing above her.

"We have to get her out of that armor," Lucas said.

"No way," Elle said. "She's getting up and going back on a different horse even if I have to—"

"Oh no you don't," Anna said, grabbing her sister's hands. "We're not going to use any magic this time. It's a joust between knights, not sisters."

"Magic!" Lucas shouted excitedly. "That's it! We can use the mace's magic to make Princess Pulverizer well again."

"No you can't." Princess Pulverizer felt tired and weak. "I haven't exactly been fighting on the side of good recently. The mace won't work on me. And its magic would be gone forever if you tried."

"Is this a trick?" Lucas asked.

"No trick," the princess promised.

"But you're so nice all of a sudden," Lucas said. "Why the switch?"

Princess Pulverizer thought for a minute. "I don't actually know," she admitted.

"It's the opal brooch," Dribble told Lucas. "She can't see it under her armor. Without that blue-and-pink stone hypnotizing her, Elle has no power over Princess Pulverizer."

"That's ridiculous. I don't have to hypnotize anyone to make them work for me," Elle insisted.

Princess Pulverizer could feel the truth-telling sword wiggle and jiggle at her side. Elle was definitely lying.

"But Princess Pulverizer was so determined to win that joust at any cost," Lucas pointed out.

"I don't think *that* had anything to do with her being hypnotized by Elle," Dribble said. "Princess Pulverizer just likes to win."

The princess didn't—*couldn't*—argue

with that one. Winning *was* important to her.

"Use the mace to cure my stallion," Princess Pulverizer insisted. "He's a good horse. It's my fault he's injured. I took too many risks."

Lucas looked over at the whimpering animal. "We have to try," he agreed.

"Okay." Dribble lifted the magical mace and waved it over the creature's injured leg.

The horse's eyes brightened. He shook his leg a bit, scrambled to his feet, and galloped off across the field.

"I told you he was a good horse," Princess Pulverizer said. She reached down and grabbed her leg. "My ankle's starting to throb."

"Don't worry, Princess. I'm getting you

out of that metal suit," Dribble said.

"Oh no!" Elle insisted. "She's getting back in the tournament. I'm not losing again."

"You'd better leave," Princess Pulverizer warned her friends. "You don't want to make Elle your enemy. I'll be okay."

"Not inside that armor you won't," Dribble said. "You shouldn't be carrying all that extra weight." He turned to Lucas. "Help me get this thing off her."

Lucas just stood there.

"Come on," Dribble urged again. "Remember, you left that whole Lucas the Lily-Livered reputation behind you. You're brave now. She's our friend. She needs our help. Besides, Anna won't let Elle hurt us."

"Of course not," Anna agreed.

Lucas took a deep breath, then bent

down to unfasten the armor from the princess's legs.

At the same time, Dribble removed the armor from her arms and upper body. As he did, the golden brooch fell onto the ground.

"Your brooch!" Elle looked at Princess Pulverizer and forced a fake smile to her lips. "Here, I'll just pin it back on and then . . ."

Before Elle could pick up the brooch, Dribble stepped on it. He turned his heavy dragon foot back and forth, grinding it into the ground. The opal stone cracked into pieces under his weight.

Dribble lifted his foot and smiled triumphantly. "Looks like your brooch— and its evil spell—are both broken."

Elle glared at Dribble. "I can't believe

you did that!" she bellowed.

"Believe it," Anna told her. "And if I were you, I'd think twice about getting back at Dribble. Remember, I have powers as strong as yours."

Elle frowned. "So now I have an *injured* knight to deal with."

"No you don't," Princess Pulverizer told her.

"You *are* injured," Dribble corrected her. "It's probably just a sprain, but . . ."

"I mean, she doesn't *have* a knight anymore," Princess Pulverizer explained. "I don't want to be a knight who ruins people's lives. I want to be a *noble* knight."

"Don't be ridiculous," Elle said. "A knight is a knight."

"That's not true," Princess Pulverizer countered. "Being a noble knight is not something you can become overnight. It takes time. And training. And if I wasn't strong enough to stand up to the magic in a little gold pin, then I'm not ready. My father was right. I have a lot to learn."

Elle rolled her eyes. "You must have hurt your head in that fall," she said. "You're speaking nonsense."

"I know exactly what I'm saying," Princess Pulverizer insisted. "I QUIT!"

"No one quits on me!" Elle shot the princess an angry look. "And you're going to be very sorry you tried."

"Don't listen to Elle," Anna said as Dribble and Lucas helped Princess Pulverizer to her feet. "You're leaving with me."

"Can you walk?" Dribble asked the princess. "Or do you need me to carry you?"

"I'm okay," Princess Pulverizer assured him. "It just hurts a little."

"You can rest in my castle," said Anna. "It's this way."

But before Princess Pulverizer could respond, she felt a piece of cloth fly into her mouth, blocking her words. She tried to pull the gag from her mouth, but already a white rope had magically tied her hands behind her back. Another rope was slithering its way around her legs, binding them so she couldn't walk.

Dribble and Lucas tried to grab their friend and rescue her. But with a single wave of Elle's hand, a locked cage appeared magically around Princess Pulverizer. She was trapped!

"Do something!" Dribble pleaded with Anna.

"I cannot undo Elle's magic," Anna admitted.

The princess gasped. Even Anna couldn't help her now.

"But I can do some magic of my own," Anna continued. She waved her hand in the air, and a key appeared magically in her palm. She reached over and quickly used it to unlock the cage. "You're free," she said kindly.

Well, not exactly. The princess was still bound and gagged by Elle's magical ropes. Anna couldn't undo those.

Which meant the princess couldn't just walk out of the cage.

But she could *hop* toward her friends. *Hop. Hop . . .*

Whoa! Just as Princess Pulverizer was about to reach her friends, she felt her feet lift off the ground.

She looked over at Elle. The wicked witch was waving her hands in the air. She was the reason the princess was flying in midair. Which would be kind of fun—if Elle weren't so evil. No good could come of this.

"I told you, nobody quits on me!" Elle exclaimed as she leaped onto her horse.

The evil witch waved her hands once again, and in an instant, the princess was hanging over the side of Elle's black-and-white mare, her head dangling over one side of the saddle and her feet over the other.

"Don't try to stop me, Anna," Elle warned. "You know what I am capable of." She kicked her horse hard in the side. "Giddyap!"

Princess Pulverizer gulped. She had no idea where they were going. But she was quite certain she wasn't going to like it there.

CHAPTER 9

"This is where you live?" Princess
Pulverizer asked nervously a little while
later as she hobbled around the castle.
Elle had taken the gag out of Princess
Pulverizer's mouth and untied her arms
and legs so she was free to move around.
But that didn't make her ankle—or the
rest of her—feel much better.

The princess had never before been
in Elle's home. Up until now, the witch

had always insisted on meeting with the princess out of doors. Which was probably just as well. This castle was awful.

"Yes, this is my home," Elle said. "And it's yours, too. Because now, instead of being my knight, you are my prisoner. You will spend every minute trapped in here. Lucky for you, I live in a really wonderful place."

Wonderful wasn't exactly the word the princess was thinking of. More like *horrifying*.

Elle's castle was decorated with velvet paintings of red-eyed rats and ravens. A real skeleton's head sat on the mantel. Above the fireplace was a giant portrait of Elle herself, with eyes that seemed to follow the princess around the room.

"This place is definitely a reflection of

your personality," the princess told Elle.

Princess Pulverizer couldn't bear the thought of staying in this horrible place much longer. But she knew she couldn't just run away. For one thing, she had an injured ankle. And for another, Elle could easily use her magic to capture her again.

An escape was going to take planning—and *patience*. So for now, the princess was going to have to get used to the skeleton skull, the creepy paintings, that doll up on the highest shelf of the bookcase, the . . .

Wait a minute. *Doll?* How strange.

The doll was beautiful, with long dark hair and smooth porcelain skin. It sure didn't fit in here.

"What a lovely doll," the princess said. She reached to take it off the shelf.

"Don't ever touch that!" Elle exclaimed

angrily. "It's mine. And no one touches it but me."

Whoa. "I never pictured you having a doll," Princess Pulverizer said.

"What, was I never a kid?" Elle asked her. "My mother gave Anna and me identical dolls. Anna's somehow ended up in the fire. But mine is still here."

The truth-telling sword by Princess Pulverizer's side began to shake. Clearly, Anna's doll didn't just "end up" in the fire. Or the doll in this room didn't belong to Elle. The princess wasn't quite sure which. She just knew Elle was lying.

"I don't care how popular Anna is," Elle continued. "She will never have a doll like that. It's irreplaceable because it came from Mother."

Wow. *That* was surprising. Not that Elle

was jealous of Anna. Jealousy was just one of Elle's many ugly traits. What was surprising was that the evil witch would be so attached to a gift. She didn't seem the sentimental type.

"I was Mother's favorite daughter," Elle boasted.

"She told you that?" the princess asked, surprised. She couldn't imagine Elle being *anyone's* favorite.

"Well, of course she couldn't *say* it," Elle continued. "But it was obvious. She gave me lovely dresses to wear, and braided my hair. She told me I was special."

Special. Well, that is definitely one way of putting it.

"Didn't your mother do those things for Anna?" Princess Pulverizer asked.

"Well, she sort of had to," Elle scoffed.

"Otherwise people would accuse her of playing favorites. But Mother was kindest to me. When no one else would play with me, Mother always did."

If the grown-up Elle was any example of what she might have been like as a child, Princess Pulverizer wasn't surprised that she didn't have many playmates.

"Wasn't your mother kind to Anna?" Princess Pulverizer replied. "Didn't she ever play with her?"

Elle let out an angry grumble. "You ask too many questions for a prisoner!"

"Elle! Set her free!" Suddenly Princess Pulverizer heard Anna's voice echo through the room.

The princess turned quickly to see the castle doors burst open. Anna, Dribble, and Lucas stormed inside.

"Boy am I glad to see you," Princess Pulverizer told her pals.

"We're here to rescue you," Lucas said, trying to sound brave, but failing miserably.

"Don't you knock?" Elle barked in her sister's direction.

Anna rushed over to her sister and

looked her straight in the eye. "I said, *set her free*."

Elle laughed in her sister's face. "You're real scary, Anna," she said sarcastically. "Now be gone, before one of your friends *somehow* winds up in the fire."

Anna's eyes went straight to the highest shelf on the bookcase. "I'm not leaving without Princess Pulverizer—and *my* doll."

"I guess you're moving in, then," Elle said. "Because you're not getting the prisoner or *my* doll."

"That's not yours," Anna insisted. "It's mine. Yours burned up in the fireplace."

"No, yours did," Elle countered.

Princess Pulverizer watched as the two sisters walked around in circles like two caged lions, readying themselves for a fight. It was impossible to tell them apart.

Was Elle the one in the blue-and-white stripes?

Or was she the one in the white-and-blue stripes?

Was there really any difference in the dresses?

"Come, Princess," one of the twin witches said. "We're leaving. There's no reason to be afraid as long as you're with me. Here, take my hand."

"Thank you, Anna." Princess Pulverizer reached for her outstretched palm.

"She's not Anna," the other witch said sweetly. "I'm Anna. Here, take *my* hand."

"Cut it out," the first witch said. "You know I'm Anna."

"No I don't," her sister insisted. "I know that *I* am Anna."

The sword of truth began to shake. But the witches were talking so quickly, the princess couldn't tell which witch the sword was calling a liar.

"Without knowing which witch is which, we won't know which way to go," said Princess Pulverizer.

"You can say that again," Lucas agreed nervously.

"I doubt it," Dribble said. "I don't know how she said it the first time."

Princess Pulverizer was very confused.

In fact, the only thing she knew for sure was that they were in trouble.

Make that *double trouble*.

CHAPTER 10

Princess Pulverizer stared at the two women in front of her. It was amazing how alike they were.

Except that wasn't completely true. Elle and Anna were only alike on the outside. Inside they were completely different. She bet Anna's castle wasn't all dark and frightening like Elle's was.

What was it she had called Elle's castle? Oh yeah, a reflection of who Elle truly was.

Wait a minute. That was it! There *was* a way to tell the difference between the twins. All she had to do was get them to the reflecting pool by the bell tower. Then Elle would see her hardened heart and turn to stone!

If only it were that easy to get the two witches to follow her to the reflecting pool. At the moment they were so focused on who owned that doll, nothing else would get them out of the dark, dingy castle.

Unless . . .

Quickly, Princess Pulverizer darted between the two feuding witches and over to the bookcase. She reached up and grabbed the porcelain doll.

"What are you doing?" one witch demanded.

"Give me my doll!" the other ordered.

"*Your* doll?" the first witch asked.

"You heard me," the second witch replied.

Princess Pulverizer started to run toward the door. But her ankle was throbbing. Running was out of the question.

"Hey, Dribble!" she called. "Think fast!" She tossed the doll in the dragon's direction.

Dribble reached out his claws and caught the doll in midair.

"Don't throw my doll!" one witch
shouted. "You'll break her."

"You mean don't throw *my* doll," the
other witch insisted.

Princess Pulverizer didn't listen. As
the two witches lunged toward Dribble,
she hobbled her way over to the doorway
and reached out her hands. "Dribble, over
here!" she shouted. "I'm clear."

"Here it comes!" Dribble exclaimed as
he tossed the doll back to her.

"I want to play!" Lucas called. He ran

past the princess and out onto the road. "Toss it to me."

As Princess Pulverizer threw the doll to Lucas, one of the witches tried to grab it. But Lucas was quick. He jumped in front of her and caught it.

"This is fun!" he said with a laugh. "Keep-away is one of my favorite games." He tossed the doll back to Dribble.

But the witches weren't playing a game. They were taking this quite seriously.

One witch waved her hand, and the doll began to fly through the air toward her.

Dribble reached up and intercepted it.

"Over here, Dribble!" Princess Pulverizer said.

Dribble tossed the doll in the princess's direction.

The second witch was quick. She waved

her hand in the air, trying to command the doll to come her way.

But Princess Pulverizer was even quicker. She leaped up on her good ankle and blocked the doll's path, catching it in her arms. Then she tossed it toward Lucas.

As the doll soared through the air, both witches began waving their arms wildly. The doll moved left. Then right. Then left. Then right. Then . . .

Dribble jumped up and grabbed the doll. He ran toward Princess Pulverizer and handed it off to her.

"What an awesome play!" Lucas cheered.

Princess Pulverizer took off as fast as her injured ankle would carry her. Despite the pain, she smiled as she ran. The princess knew that by working together, she and her friends would surely get Elle to that reflecting pool. It was all about teamwork. Something Elle and Anna had never mastered.

"Over here, Princess Pulverizer!" Lucas shouted as he moved to the water's edge.

Princess Pulverizer threw the doll at Lucas.

One witch used her magic to draw the flying doll toward her.

The other witch used *her* magic to direct the flying doll toward *her*.

Lucas jumped between them. "I got it!" he shouted, reaching his hands high. "I got . . ."

The doll hit the tips of Lucas's fingers, knocking it out of the paths of the two witches. It flew a little farther through the air and then . . .

SPLASH! It plopped down in the reflecting pool.

"I *don't* got it," Lucas said with a frown.

"My doll!" one of the witches shouted out in dismay.

"She's gone!" the other witch sobbed as she ran over to the reflecting pool. Without thinking, she looked down into the water.

A moment later, her fingers curled like a tiger's claws.

Her feet hardened like lead.

And her skin turned gray as slate.

"You! You horrible Princess Pulverizer! What have you done to me?"

Those were the last words anyone ever heard from Elle, the evil witch of Starats. For a moment later, even her tongue had turned to stone.

CHAPTER 11

"No skin. No bone. Evil Elle has turned to stone!"

Word spread quickly that someone had finally forced Elle to look at her true self in the reflecting pool. The people of Starats had come running to see the proof. And now they were cheering in the streets.

The crowd was overjoyed to see the life-size Elle statue near the pool of water. At least until they realized the statue was solid stone and not going anywhere.

"I don't want to have to pass by a statue of Elle every time I come to the reflecting pool," said the boy who had been bitten by the cookie.

"Me either," the strawberry farmer agreed. "I say knock it down."

"Knock it down!" Millie cheered.

"Knock it down!" Lily echoed.

But Anna shook her head. "No, my friends. We can't just knock this down."

"Why not?" the bagpipe player asked her.

"Elle was my sister," Anna said. "I feel bad that she never learned how good it feels to be kind. But I don't want to forget that she ever existed. I have an idea."

Anna waved her hands in the air. A moment later, a second stone statue appeared beside the one of Elle. It showed Princess Pulverizer standing bravely beside Dribble and Lucas.

"Hey! That's us!" Princess Pulverizer exclaimed.

"We look pretty good," Dribble said.

"We sure do," Lucas agreed proudly.

"These statues will stand side by side to remind the people of Starats that good will always triumph over evil," Anna explained.

"Hip hip hooray!" the crowd shouted. "Three cheers for our three heroes!"

"We wish to give you a token of our gratitude," Anna told Princess Pulverizer and her friends.

"How about this sock?" Lily suggested, pulling a wet sock from her bucket.

"It has only one hole," Millie added. "And it doesn't smell *too* bad."

Anna laughed. "Actually, I was thinking of this hand mirror," she said, handing Princess Pulverizer a gold-and-silver mirror. "Its magic is powerful. You can see the future reflected in the glass."

"Thank you. That will come in very handy," Princess Pulverizer said.

"If we see a monster in the mirror, we will know to get away quickly," Lucas suggested.

"Or know that we should stay and fight it," Princess Pulverizer countered.

"Take heed," Anna warned. "The future you see in the mirror may not turn out exactly the way you think it will."

"Right now, the reflection in the mirror is of our backs as we walk down the road," Princess Pulverizer pointed out.

"Well, *I'm* walking. You two seem to be dancing," she told Dribble and Lucas.

"I guess that means we are leaving Starats in the near future," Dribble said.

"I guess so," Anna replied with a smile. "Thank you again."

"This silly song has no beginning.
It goes on without an end.
You sing it high. You sing it low.
Then start it once again.
This silly song has no beginning.
It goes on without an end—"

"Is that a real song?" Princess Pulverizer interrupted Dribble as he sang.

The three friends were traveling in search of a new adventure. Dribble and

Lucas were dancing while the princess walked—just as the mirror had predicted.

"Well, it's a *song*," Dribble answered. "And I'm *really* singing it."

"I like it," Lucas said. He began to sing.

Well, there's no rule that says a Quest of Kindness can't be fun, Princess Pulverizer thought. And if she couldn't beat 'em, she might as well join 'em. She opened her mouth and began to sing.

Dribble and Lucas stared at Princess Pulverizer with surprise. Not that she blamed them. The princess herself was pretty surprised to be singing. No magic mirror could ever have predicted *that*!

Still, many strange things had happened on the Quest of Kindness. And with three more good deeds to go, stranger things were sure to come.

PRINCESS PULVERIZER

coLLect each adventure on your reading quest!

author & illustrator

Nancy Krulik

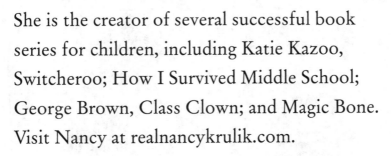

is the author of more than two hundred books for children and young adults, including three *New York Times* Best Sellers.

She is the creator of several successful book series for children, including Katie Kazoo, Switcheroo; How I Survived Middle School; George Brown, Class Clown; and Magic Bone. Visit Nancy at realnancykrulik.com.

Justin Rodrigues

is a character designer and visual development artist based in Los Angeles, California. He has worked for acclaimed studios including DreamWorks Animation, Disney Television Animation, Marvel, Fisher-Price, and many more.